Adventures in Extreme Reading

#5

BIG CITY BLUES

BACK TO WONDERLAND

BY Jan Fields

magic wagon

visit us at www.abdopublishing.com

Published by Magic Wagon, a division of the ABDO Group,
PO Box 398166, Minneapolis, MN 55439. Copyright © 2013 by
Abdo Consulting Group, Inc. International copyrights reserved in all
countries. All rights reserved. No part of this book may be reproduced
in any form without written permission from the publisher.

Calico Chapter Books™ is a trademark and logo of Magic Wagon.

Printed in the United States of America, North Mankato, Minnesota.
102012
012013
♻ This book contains at least 10% recycled materials.

Written by Jan Fields
Cover illustration by Scott Altmann
Edited by Stephanie Hedlund and Grace Hansen
Cover and interior design by Neil Klinepier

Library of Congress Cataloging-in-Publication Data

Fields, Jan.
  Big city blues : back to Wonderland / by Jan Fields ; [illustrator, Scott
Altmann].
     p. cm. -- (Adventures in extreme reading ; bk. 5)
  Summary: Uncle Dan Hunter is taking his virtual reality program
public, and thirteen-year old Carter and his cousin Isabelle are helping
him demonstrate the suits at a children's bookstore--but when a
blackout fuses Wind in the willows with Peter Pan, Carter has battle
pirates and weasels to rescue the two children trapped in the suits.
  ISBN 978-1-61641-923-3
1. Virtual reality--Juvenile fiction. 2. Books and reading--Juvenile
fiction. 3. Children's literature--Juvenile fiction. 4. Inventions--
Juvenile fiction. 5. Cousins--Juvenile fiction. 6. Uncles--Juvenile
fiction. [1. Virtual reality--Fiction. 2. Books and reading--Fiction.
3. Inventions--Fiction. 4. Cousins--Fiction. 5. Uncles--Fiction.] I.
Altmann, Scott, ill. II. Title.
  PZ7.F479177Big 2013
  813.6--dc23
                                              2012028633

Table of Contents

THE BIG REVEAL

Carter reached out and felt around for his cell phone on the desk by his bed. He opened his eyes to slits, trying not to let too much morning in. Finally, his hand hit the phone.

"Who is texting at dawn on a school-free Friday?" he grumbled as he held the phone close to his nose to read it.

The first thing he noticed was that it was ten o'clock. *Okay*, he thought, *dawn came and went a while ago . . .*

Carter blinked as he tried to make sense of the message. It was from Uncle Dan and looked like random numbers and letters: a9i9/3o19e21o35.

Carter moaned. There was no way he could

4

do this one in his head. He'd need paper. That meant getting up.

He closed his eyes for a moment, wondering what would happen if he just pretended he hadn't heard the phone. He could go back to sleep. Then his stomach grumbled.

"Okay, okay," he muttered as he sat up. He swung his long legs over the side of the bed.

Carter copied the letters and numbers onto a sheet of paper. It was obviously a code. Uncle Dan loved codes. They fed his need for security and offered a mental challenge. Uncle Dan was always in favor of a mental challenge.

Carter figured this was probably some kind of substitution code. In a substitution code, some or all of the letters are replaced by numbers. Immediately he noticed that all the letters in the code were vowels. That meant the code might only represent consonants.

Carter chewed his lip as he studied the paper. He wrote out the most common substitution code that only used consonants:

B/1 C/2 D/3 F/4 G/5 H/6 J/7 K/8 L/9
M/10 N/11 P/12 Q/13 R/14 S/15 T/16
V/17 W/18 X/19 Y/20 Z/21

Carter saw the problem with that right away. The numbers in the code from his phone went much higher than 21. He squinted as he studied the numbers, looking for a pattern. He spotted it quickly. They were all odd numbers. Carter rewrote his replacement code using only odd numbers.

B/1 C/3 D/5 F/7 G/9 H/11 J/13 K/15
L/17 M/19 N/21 P/23 Q/25 R/27 S/29
T/31 V/33 W/35 X/37 Y/39 Z/41

Now the code worked for the original message. Carter wrote it out quickly: agigcomenow. He grinned as he broke it into words and added punctuation: "A gig. Come now!"

Uncle Dan must have set a date for the first public use of his virtual reality suits. Finally, they were going to be able to show other people how cool it was to enter a virtual reality world based on a book.

Carter thought about the last few weeks as he pulled on a pair of jeans. After they'd finally caught the hacker who wanted to destroy Uncle Dan's invention, the finishing touches on the project went fast. Then Uncle Dan had looked for a place to exhibit the finished product.

When his stomach grumbled again, Carter decided he'd better feed the beast before dashing off to Uncle Dan's house. When he hit the kitchen, he spotted the green and white box on the counter. "Yes! Doughnuts!"

He flipped the lid back and scowled. There were mostly raspberry jelly doughnuts, yuck. He nudged aside two plain cake doughnuts, boring. Then he found a lone chocolate and snagged it.

Uncle Dan would just have to fill the rest of his junk food needs. As he hauled open the front door, he heard his mom's voice. "Is that you, Carter?"

"Yesph," he said around a mouthful.

"Your dad wants you to mow the lawn."

Carter sagged against the door frame and quickly swallowed. "I got a text from Uncle Dan. He needs me. Can I do the lawn when I get back?"

"Will Isabelle be there?"

Carter groaned. His parents adored his brainy cousin. "Yeah, I'm sure she will."

"Good," his mom called back. "See if she has some time to help you with that algebra that stumped your dad."

Another groan. "Okay. Can I go?"

"Yes, go, go. But don't forget the lawn."

"Thanks, Mom." Carter had the door closed by the time he said *Mom*. He would have to do the lawn, but he believed in putting off any hot, sweaty tasks as long as possible.

When he turned up the drive to his uncle's house, he could see Isabelle's bike peeking out from behind the trash can corral. Though they lived about the same distance away, Izzy always beat Carter to the house. Either that, or she sat outside Uncle Dan's just waiting for a call.

Carter wouldn't put anything past her.

Uncle Dan answered the door in a purple party hat. He plunked a matching one on Carter's head and blew a roll-out noisemaker at him.

"We're celebrating," he said.

"You got a place to demonstrate the suits?" Carter asked as soon as he slipped the goofy hat off his head.

"Yes, a children's bookstore in the city," Uncle Dan said. "It's called Alice's Wonders. They have a special room for author presentations that will work perfectly. We're on for next weekend."

Uncle Dan had led the way to the kitchen where Isabelle leaned against the counter. She wore two of the kids' hats, giving her the look of horns.

"Do you think you can avoid being grounded for a week?" Izzy asked. "You don't want to leave Uncle Dan shorthanded."

"I can manage," Carter grumbled. He turned to his uncle. "What exactly will you need us to do?" He imagined climbing into one of the virtual reality suits to take kids on a magical tour of some kids' book. He wasn't crazy about little kids, but he'd grown to love the book adventures, even when they tried to kill him. He thought of it as "extreme reading."

"Mostly tote and fetch," Uncle Dan said. "We need to get all of my equipment into the room and set up. I only have the two fully functional suits and I'm going to put kids in both of them. I'm taking a backup just in case, but I don't plan to use it. It's one of the prototypes."

"One that made you throw up?" Carter said.

"Um, yes." Uncle Dan clapped his hands and rubbed them together. "This is so exciting. Once a few kids find out what an amazing way this is to experience a book, every bookstore in the country will want this setup."

Isabelle giggled and Carter turned to stare at her. His cousin never giggled. She snarked. She scoffed. On a good day she smiled, but she never giggled. He'd never seen Izzy or Uncle

Dan so wired.

Carter leaned close to his cousin and whispered, "Why are you so excited?"

"Aren't you?" She stared at him, surprise clear on her face. "We worked so hard to deal with that hacker. This proves we won. Storm wanted to ruin everything, but we won."

Carter nodded. That was great, but somehow he just didn't feel all giggly about it. Mostly he was disappointed that his job was going to be schlepping equipment and watching strange kids get into the suits instead of him.

"So are you just going to be carrying equipment, too?" he asked Izzy.

She shrugged. "Mostly. But I'll be on the computers too, in case Uncle Dan needs more than one set of hands."

That made sense. As usual, Isabelle was the one Uncle Dan couldn't do without. Carter knew it was a little childish to be jealous of Isabelle. It's not like Carter wanted to be a computer nerd. Still, he felt jealous.

"Besides celebrating," Carter said, raising his voice to include his uncle, "are we here for anything else?"

"Definitely," Uncle Dan said. He reached up and pulled the paper hat from his head. "And I'm glad you want to move on, because I have a ton of equipment to pack up. To the lab!"

"To the lab!" Isabelle echoed.

"Yeah, right," Carter added weakly. "Charge."

He trudged down the stairs behind the others. The inside of Uncle Dan's lab looked messier than usual. Cables lay in piles. Keyboards perched awkwardly on top of computer monitors. When Carter peeked into the suit room, he saw both of the suits had been taken down. They lay in collapsed piles on the floor, as if someone had just deflated two astronauts.

Packing up all the gear was about as exciting as Carter had expected. Uncle Dan had a kind of crazy system that made sense to him but looked like total chaos to Carter's ultraorganized cousin. Isabelle kept switching things from one box to another.

"This is better," she insisted.

Uncle Dan didn't argue with her. He simply went along behind her and switched everything back. Eventually, the chaos got to be a little too much for Carter.

"I need to get home and mow the lawn," Carter announced. He was suddenly aware that he'd never looked forward to lawn mowing before.

"No problem," Uncle Dan said as he dumped an armload of equipment into a box. "Just be here next Saturday by six."

"Six?" Carter yelped. "I'm pretty sure it's against the law to get up before six on a Saturday."

Uncle Carter grinned. "We'll just have to live dangerously. Isn't that fantastic?" Then he ducked his head back in the box and began rooting around. Carter gave up with a defeated sigh. He headed back up the steps to go home and face the crabgrass.

ALICE'S WONDERS

When the special day finally rolled around, Carter was on his bike and heading to his uncle's house as the sun peeked over the horizon.

"This is so wrong," he muttered. Only a few weeks stood between him and summer break. Carter was beginning to suspect that Uncle Dan's project might mean a lot of mornings where he got to watch the sun rise.

As Carter turned up the drive to Uncle Dan's, he spotted Isabelle carrying a box out to a van. "You're late," she yelled.

Carter snuck a glance at his wrist. No, he wasn't. "You're early!"

"The early bird gets the worm," she said.

Carter hopped off his bike and walked it

toward the trash cans. He called out, "I'll stick to cereal. You can have the worms."

When he reached the front door, Uncle Dan shoved a box into his arms. Just when Carter thought his arms might fall off, they finished loading.

"Shotgun!" Carter whooped and raced Isabelle to the van. With his longer legs, she didn't stand a chance.

"Carter," Uncle Dan yelled, "let Isabelle sit up front. She's better at navigating."

"What navigating?" Carter asked. "You've got GPS!"

"I don't always do what it says," Uncle Dan said cheerily. "It gets too bossy."

"Fine," Carter grumbled. "I'll just sleep back here." And he did, nodding off almost before they got out of the neighborhood. He didn't wake up until Isabelle hit him on the head with a wadded up granola bar wrapper.

"We're here, Rip Van Winkle," she said. She paused before adding, "He was a character in a story by Washington Irving . . ."

"I know," Carter said. "The guy who slept for years and woke up to find everything different. I read too, you know."

The truth was that he'd only been reading since Uncle Dan started his project. After being trapped in "The Legend of Sleepy Hollow" and *Great Expectations*, Carter firmly believed that what you didn't know could hurt you!

"Okay, no fighting," Uncle Dan said. "We want to make a good impression."

Isabelle and Carter both agreed. When Carter scrambled out, he got his first glimpse of the bookstore. It was a huge brick building. Black silhouettes of characters from *Alice in Wonderland* decorated the tall windows. Carter shuddered, remembering his time spent running from characters in that story after the hacker had rewritten part of the program code. He could still hear the sound of the March Hare's steel teeth.

A tall woman with short, black hair and a

wide smile stood near the doors of the store. When Uncle Dan climbed out of the van, she hurried over, calling his name. Uncle Dan thrust out his hand.

"You must be Alice Millhouse," he said. "It's nice to meet you after chatting so much on the phone, Miss Millhouse."

Miss Millhouse fluttered her hands. "Please, call me Alice."

"If you'll call me Dan."

All the smiling and fluttering was making Carter nervous. The last time Uncle Dan had gotten goofy over a woman, Carter ended up being chased through the streets of Victorian London by a man with a knife. Okay, it was only virtual Victorian London, but with the magic of Uncle Dan's virtual reality suits, bad guys could still give bruises.

"Should we start carrying in boxes?" Carter asked.

"Oh, yes, of course." More fluttering followed. Uncle Dan kept smiling. Ick.

Carter trudged to the back of the van and hauled out a box of cables. Isabelle grabbed another box.

"Uncle Dan is losing it again," he whispered.

"I think he's just humoring her," Isabelle whispered back.

Miss Millhouse led them through the empty store to a large alcove. "You can set up here," she said. "I brought in some folding tables for your electronics and had the ceiling panels removed like you asked."

Uncle Dan nodded as he looked up. "That should be a large enough area to hang the suits." He grabbed the box from Carter and began pulling out cables without a word.

Carter sighed and walked back out to the van for another load. When he carried it in, Uncle Dan was already up on a ladder and Carter spotted Isabelle above him in the ceiling.

"Why couldn't I go in the ceiling?" he asked.

"Isabelle's lighter," Uncle Dan said. "And better with wiring."

Since he couldn't argue with either point, Carter dropped his box on the closest folding table and headed back out to the van. He felt like a pack mule as he carried in the rest of the boxes.

He had to give Uncle Dan and Isabelle credit, they worked fast. Each time he carried in a new box, the room looked a little different. By the time Carter dropped the last box next to the table, one of the suits hung from the ceiling like a giant astronaut marionette.

"Oh, I don't need that box," Uncle Dan said. "It's the spare suit."

"You want me to take it back to the van?" Carter asked.

Uncle Dan shook his head. "Don't bother. Just put it in the corner. I've dropped cable for it, just in case, but I'm sure we won't need it."

Carter considered suggesting his uncle not say things like that. In the movies, every time a character said everything was fine or they wouldn't have a problem, *bam*, trouble hit.

Instead, he said, "That's the last box. What do I need to do now?"

Uncle Dan looked up. "Um, I think we're okay for now. You can look around if you want."

Carter saw Isabelle untangling cords as she hooked up another computer. Carter suddenly felt like he wore a big "doofy kid" sticker. He walked out of the alcove and flopped on the first overstuffed chair he found.

He knew he wasn't all that good with computers, and he didn't want to be. He was perfectly happy for Izzy to hold the job of family nerd. Still, he'd helped a lot in getting the program ready. Who had beaten the hacker time after time from inside the books? Him. Okay, with help from Isabelle, but still, he was the adventure guy. He was the one who sorted out the disasters.

"No disasters today," he muttered. Then he felt a nudge of nerves. He'd just done it. He'd done the movie thing. He looked around, half-expecting a massive disaster to rain down on them now that he'd said it. But it was still just a big empty bookstore. So he slumped deeper in the chair and let his eyes glaze over while he watched Uncle Dan and Isabelle work.

He jumped when someone put a hand on his arm. He was on his feet in a second. "What? What?" he asked.

"Sorry, I didn't mean to scare you." A girl about his age offered him a foam cup. "Aunt Alice said to see if you wanted something, so I got you a chai latte."

Carter wasn't totally sure what a chai latte was, but he didn't want to admit it. "Thanks. I guess I fell asleep."

"It looks like they're almost done," she said. "Everything looks so cool, like a scene from a science fiction movie."

Carter followed her gaze. Both suits now hung from the ceiling in a web of cables. The cables carried information to and from the suits and the computers on the tables.

The mass of cables that trailed around on

the floor in Uncle Dan's lab had been neatly bundled and taped down to reduce any chance of someone tripping. In fact, the whole setup was much neater. Uncle Dan wasn't exactly known for neatness, so Carter knew that was Isabelle's influence. She was a total neat freak.

Carter took a sip from the cup the girl had handed him. It was sweet and spicy. Suddenly, he realized he was being rude.

"Oh, I'm Carter," he said to the girl.

She nodded. "Aunt Alice told me. I'm Amber. I hope I get a chance to try this out. You've probably been in the suits a ton of times."

Carter nodded.

Her eyes widened. "Really? What books have you been in? I think that's so cool, getting to be inside a book. I would love to go inside *Twilight*."

Carter winced. All he knew about *Twilight* could be summed up with "sparkly vampires."

"So far, Uncle Dan's only used classics to test the suits," he said. "So I've been in *The Three*

Musketeers, Treasure Island, 'The Legend of Sleepy Hollow,' and a bunch of others."

"That must have been wonderful," she said.

"Well," he answered, "it was during testing so some of the books weren't exactly the way they were written."

"Oh, like with computer glitches?" she asked.

"Something like that." Carter and Amber both jumped when Uncle Dan spoke from right beside them. How did he sneak up on them like that? Carter felt his face warm as he realized just how much he'd been distracted by his conversation with Amber. He was getting as goofy as Uncle Dan over girls.

"So, who do we have here?" Uncle Dan asked in a cheery voice that made Carter cringe.

"I'm Amber Millhouse," Amber said.

"Alice's daughter?" Uncle Dan asked.

"Niece."

"Ah, I totally approve of nieces and nephews helping out! I'd be lost without Izzy and Carter. Which reminds me, it's time to test the system.

Are you ready to suit up, Carter?"

Carter blinked in surprise. He hadn't known he was going to get in the suits at all. "Yeah!"

"Lucky," Amber teased. "I would love to try."

"Really?" Uncle Dan said. "Well, if it's okay with your aunt, then you're welcome to suit up, too. I need Izzy on the computers so you'll be doing me a favor by testing the other suit."

"I'll go ask," Amber said, already spinning on her heel to run up the aisle. She shouted, "Aunt Alice!"

Uncle Dan laughed. "That's what I like. Eager assistants!"

Carter followed Uncle Dan into the alcove and headed toward one of the suits. "What book are we testing?" he asked.

"We'll let Amber choose," Uncle Dan said. "I only brought a few though—mostly kids' books. I tried to stay away from anything that could get violent."

A breathless Amber ran into the alcove. "Aunt Alice said it would be fine."

"Great," Uncle Dan said. "Let's look at your choices." He handed Amber a printout of the available books.

"Oh, these are really old," Amber said. "But I loved *Anne of Green Gables*."

Carter repressed a moan, *girly book*.

"Oh, *Little Women*!"

Carter shuddered, *mega-girly book*.

"Wait, this one." She pointed at the sheet of paper and looked up at Uncle Dan with a bright smile. "I definitely want to do that one."

Izzy had stepped over to see which one Amber chose. She looked at Carter, grinned, and announced, "*Alice in Wonderland* it is!"

This time Carter didn't bother to stifle the moan. Another trip down the rabbit hole, just perfect.

BACK TO WONDERLAND

Carter took a few deep breaths, then he climbed into the suit. The total darkness that pressed on him as soon as the back of the suit was closed always made him feel a little panicky.

"Can you both hear me?" Uncle Dan's voice asked in his right ear.

"Yes," Amber chirped. Her voice was so close it was as if she were whispering in his ear. It was a creepy feeling in the darkness of the suit.

"I hear you," Carter said. His voice sounded shaky, so he cleared his throat and added, "Whenever you're ready."

"Okay, here we go."

Light exploded around him, making Carter stagger a moment, blinking. He looked around and saw Amber standing a few feet to his left, staring with wide eyes.

"I can't believe this," she said. "It's so clear. And . . ." She took a deep breath. "It smells like a park."

"Great," Uncle Dan's voice said. "So the scents are working. How about you, Carter? Do you smell anything?"

Carter took a deep breath. "She's right. It smells like outdoors. And I feel a little breeze."

"Excellent! Well, we'll run through a scene or two, so you two better go find a rabbit."

"About those rabbits . . .," Carter said to Amber. "Be careful. They can be scary."

She looked at him blankly for a second.

"Trust me."

Just then, a familiar white rabbit in a vest burst from between two trees and ran by them. Directly after, a young girl followed.

"I can't believe it," Amber said. "It's Alice and the White Rabbit. Aren't they adorable?"

"Yeah," Carter said. "Whatever you do, don't

let her hold your hand."

Amber gave him another funny look, then she turned and dashed off. Carter sighed and ran after her. He knew it wasn't her fault. She hadn't been in this book when all the characters were out to kill him.

They raced after the pair until they disappeared into a hedge. "Be careful here," Carter said. "There's a hole on the other side."

Amber rolled her eyes. "I know that. I've read this book a dozen times." She pushed through the hedge and Carter followed. As soon as she reached the deep hole in the ground, she jumped in without pausing.

Carter looked down into the hole. "Haven't we tested the system enough?" he asked.

Izzy spoke in his ear. "Aw, let your girlfriend have a little fun."

"Hey," Carter whispered, "she's not my girlfriend!"

"No fighting," Uncle Dan said. "Just go on, Carter. I want to see some scene changes."

"Right, sure," Carter said, then he stepped off into space. He remembered the slow-motion falling from the last time he'd been in the book. He hoped it would work the same way now.

Carter passed shelves of things embedded into the walls of the hole. He looked them over, but this time none of the objects had anything to do with storms or weather.

Finally, he landed with a soft thud at the bottom of the hole and stood up. He was facing a long hall. Amber was halfway down the hall, peering behind a curtain.

"Come and see this," she squeaked. "It's the rose garden."

Carter walked over and knelt beside her. The tiny door gave them a glimpse into a lovely miniature garden of white roses. Carter could even smell the roses through the open door.

"How did you get it open?" he asked. "Wasn't it locked?"

"I've read this book," she said. "I knew how to get in." She sighed. "I wish we were staying long enough to see the gardeners painting the roses. They must be so funny."

"They were a little funny," Carter admitted.

Amber opened her eyes wide. "You've been in this book before?"

Carter nodded. "It had some problems then. I can see Uncle Dan fixed all the glitches."

"It's perfect," she said, turning to look around the hall again. "Let's go for a swim!"

"Swim?" Carter asked weakly.

Amber just grinned. She walked down the hall to the glass table Carter knew well. She picked up a small bottle with a paper tag. Carter knew from experience that the tag said, "Drink me!"

"I'm not sure that's a good idea," he said, hurrying down the hall toward her.

She just smiled and tipped the bottle up to her lips. She began to shrink just as Carter reached her side. He took the bottle and drained the last drops. He certainly couldn't let her face the next part alone.

They shrank quickly. The table top seemed to rush toward him, then as he kept shrinking, the underside of the table vanished in the distance. He and Amber had been standing right beside one another. As they shrunk, he lost sight of her, too. He soon found himself treading water in a salty pool.

"Amber!" he shouted. "Where are you?"

Carter didn't get an answer, so he picked a direction and began swimming. He soon saw other creatures paddling along in the water, but he knew he needed to find Amber. She might know the book, but he knew how this whole virtual reality thing worked. And, Carter knew exactly how hurt you could get in here.

He spotted Amber's dark head above the water, swimming behind Alice. He felt a surge of relief. Alice would lead her to the shore. Carter swam toward them, catching up easily.

"What took you so long?" Amber sputtered as he took his place beside her.

"Took the scenic route," he said.

They reached the edge of the pool and scrambled out on a rocky shore. "This didn't make sense to me last time," Carter said.

"What?" Amber asked as she wrung out her wet hair.

"We were in a hallway. So where did this shoreline come from?"

Amber laughed. "*Alice in Wonderland* is a dream, Carter. When did dreams ever make sense?"

Isabelle had used the same argument on him, but Carter still felt grumpy. It might be a dream, but it was also a book. Books were supposed to make sense in his opinion.

Amber was scanning the group of animals around them. "Oh look!" She reached out and grabbed his arm as she pointed. "It's the Dodo!"

"Wowie," he said, then felt bad when she glared at him.

"This was my favorite book ever since my Aunt Alice read it to me when I was little," she said. "You could try to enjoy it."

"It's a pretty creepy book to read to a little kid," he said. "There's a woman in here who wants to cut off people's heads. And there's a crazy hatter. And that cat—that thing has way too many teeth."

Her frown slipped away at the mention of the cat. "You've seen the Cheshire Cat? Oh, I've always wanted to see the Cheshire Cat. Where is it?"

"As I remember, when all these animals went nuts and tried to kill me, I ran away with Alice hanging on to me," he said. "She's a very creepy little kid, by the way. And we ended up in the woods. That's where I saw the cat."

The animals around them began to argue over the best way to dry off. A mouse launched into a speech about the Earl of Northumbria. Last time the speech was full of stuff about storms, but this time it was just dull.

"Oh, well, they're going to have a race here in a minute," Amber said, looking around. "But it's not my favorite part. Maybe we should try running away? We would dry off and maybe see the cat?" She held out her hand.

Carter liked the idea of drying off. "Okay, let's go for it." Then he reached out and took her hand. Together they turned away and ran.

Amber kept up a lot better than Alice had. Carter found he actually liked holding her hand—a little bit. The slope soon climbed into a stretch of woods that Carter recognized. He slowed to a walk.

"The cat was around here last time."

"How exciting," Amber said. She spun in a slow circle peering into the trees. "Cheshire Cat? Are you there?"

"No." A deep, smooth voice spoke from above them. "I am here. You are there."

"I'm so glad to meet you," Amber said.

The cat blinked at her and yawned, showing off the long, sharp teeth Carter remembered. He leaned closer to Amber and whispered, "Is it supposed to have teeth like that?"

"They are much more useful than the short

stumps in your mouth," the cat said sulkily.

"It's a cat," Amber said. "Even real cats have pointy teeth. What is it with you? I thought you were supposed to be some kind of adventurer."

"Hey, I've had plenty of adventures," he said.

"Really?" she snapped. "'Cause you seem like a big chicken now."

"Hey, just because I'm not starstruck by a stupid cat."

"Okay, guys," Uncle Dan's voice interrupted. "I think we have enough test data. The program is working. You two can come out now."

"Now you've ruined it," Amber said.

"What? We were just testing the system. We were never going to stay in here!"

"Lucky for you, chicken boy."

Just then, everything went dark. For once, Carter was almost glad of the tight closeness of the dark suit. He'd had more than enough female company for one day.

SHOWTIME

Amber thanked Uncle Dan, then she stomped out of the alcove.

"You make friends wherever you go," Isabelle said to Carter.

"She's crazy," he snapped.

"We know the system is online and working," Uncle Dan said. "That's what matters."

"Right," Carter mumbled as he walked to the corner of the alcove and flopped back on a chair. Now there was nothing to do but sit around and be bored.

Alice Millhouse walked up just then. She smiled brightly. "It's time to open. There is already a line out there! Are you ready?"

Uncle Dan grinned at her. "You know it. Remember, since this is our test run, we're giving the kids thirty minutes in the suits."

"No problem," she said. "I'm putting my niece on the registration table and she has a chart with 40-minute slots to give you some extra time for any setting up you might need."

"Sounds perfect."

"Good. Well, I better go open the doors, I didn't want to leave them outside a moment more than necessary. It's getting horribly hot out. It's hard to believe it's not even officially summer yet."

Uncle Dan winced in sympathy. "It's always hotter in the city."

She nodded, then she smiled again and hurried off to let in the customers. Within minutes, a group of parents and children filled the small alcove. Some already held tickets, while others just wanted to look at the dangling virtual reality suits.

Uncle Dan had to shoo children away from touching the suits and trying to climb the cables. Finally, he called Carter over to police the kids.

"I don't want to spend half the day

reattaching cables," Uncle Dan said.

Carter grumbled a bit about daycare duty, but he took his place quickly. He didn't want the kids tearing the suits up either. Plus, it was more interesting to be the suit policeman than to sit and watch the computer screens. Carter hadn't realized just how much better it was to be in the suits than to be outside watching.

The first kids in the suit were a pair of twin girls with matching jumpers. When Uncle Dan asked them which book they wanted, they answered together. "Harry Potter!"

"Oh, girls," a stout woman with frizzy curls laughed nervously. "I told you they don't have Harry Potter. They want to try out *Secret Garden*." Her face turned dreamy. "It was my favorite book as a child."

The twins' faces scrunched up into matching looks of disgust. "Does it have magic?"

"It's very magical," their mother answered.

The girls looked at one another and finally nodded. Uncle Dan hustled them to the suits and explained that it would be dark inside at first, but would quickly brighten as the story started.

"You'll see, hear, feel, and smell the story," he said.

"Can you taste it?" one twin asked. "I always wanted to taste real Bertie Botts Every Flavor Beans."

"That's Harry Potter," her twin said. "This is some book Mom likes."

"Oh right," she said. "Will there be any magical things to eat?"

"I don't want to spoil the surprise," Uncle Dan said. He practically shoved the first girl into the suit. Carter began to suspect Uncle Dan was going to find the day a lot more stressful than he expected.

Carter had never watched a suit in use before. The suits twitched and wheezed. The girls made them walk even though their feet dangled about a foot above the floor. With the blacked out visors of the suits, they looked like squirming aliens. Carter couldn't decide if it was creepy or really cool.

Seeing the suits move as the story played out was so interesting that the thirty minutes passed quickly. Finally, Uncle Dan called, "Time. Get the kids out of there."

Isabelle walked to one suit and Carter stepped over to the other. On the way, he gave a fierce glare to a little boy who had tried to climb the cables three times.

"I'm watching you," he said, using his best scary voice. The boy simply stuck out his tongue.

When Carter opened the back of the suit, the little girl tumbled out into his arms. "That was the coolest thing ever," she said. "Even without magic wands."

"I think the bird might have been magic," the other twin said as Isabelle helped her down to the floor. "Remember how it showed us the key to the garden?"

"Maybe," her sister said. "Though I think Dickon was more magic than the robin."

Carter wasn't sure what the girls were talking about, but he was glad they had a good time. The next two kids rushed at Uncle Dan, ready to take their turn.

Carter fiddled with the open back of the suit while the two little boys argued over which book they would choose. Finally, their mother made the choice for them and both boys were ready to try out *Treasure Island*.

"You'll like that one," Carter told the boy he helped into the suit. "I've been in that one. The pirates are cool."

"Are they mean?" the boy asked eagerly. "And scary."

"Both."

The boy grinned and scrambled into the suit. As Carter sealed it, he hoped Uncle Dan put the kids in the book somewhere in the middle so they could be on the pirate ship, or maybe on the island.

Of course the boys would be there to have fun in the book. When Carter had spent his time in *Treasure Island*, he was desperately trying to find the hacker and save Uncle Dan. Maybe he'd ask Uncle Dan for a chance to go in the book again sometime, just for fun.

The boys were soon followed by another pair of girls who wanted to spend some time in *Anne of Green Gables*. Carter had to keep shooing kids away from the cables, but he still got bored. The fun of watching the suits squirm and twitch had passed. Now he just wished the day would end so he could go home.

Carter noticed that Miss Millhouse brought Uncle Dan several cups of coffee, but Amber never came back at all. He looked through the group of moms and kids, hoping to see Amber looking back at him. Then he heard a rumble of thunder vibrate through the store.

Carter hoped the rain would cool things down by the time they had to pack all the stuff up. One of the mothers voiced the same hope for a break in the heat.

"I doubt it," another mom said. "This summer

has been roasting. The storms just seem to push the heat down."

The other woman nodded wearily. "At least they have air-conditioning here."

The first woman looked around. "As long as we don't get a brownout."

Carter knew the city got a lot of brownouts when the weather was really hot. Too many air-conditioners meant it was tough for the electric company to meet the demand as the temperatures climbed.

His attention was pulled back to the job when Uncle Dan called for him to help the kids out of the suits.

"Okay, everyone," Uncle Dan said to the waiting group. "We're going to take a fifteen minute break."

A groan from the moms and the kids echoed around the alcove. "Sorry, guys," Uncle Dan said sheepishly. "I had a little too much coffee."

He turned to Isabelle. "Help Carter keep the kids off the suits. If you guys need to run to the restroom, take turns. Don't leave the suits alone."

"No problem," Isabelle said as she walked over to stand beside Carter. She looked sharply at a boy creeping slowly toward the boot of the closest suit. The little boy took a quick step backward.

"Wow," Carter said. "They don't back off when I look at them."

"You need to perfect your evil glare," Isabelle said. "So, what's up with you anyway?"

"Up?"

"Well, you're always good at complaining," she said, "but you seem more miserable than usual."

"Thanks." Carter scuffed the toe of his sneaker on the carpet in the alcove. "You know," he said. "I'm really glad Uncle Dan is having such a great day."

"I know," Isabelle said, nodding. "But?"

"I guess I don't feel very useful. When we were dealing with that hacker, I had a job to do. It was scary, but important. Now I'm just carrying boxes and babysitting." He sighed. "You're still important, but Uncle Carter could hire a monkey to do my job."

"Since I'm feeling kind," Isabelle said with a smirk, "I'm not going to suggest you are a monkey." She held up her hand before Carter could say anything. "And keeping these little monkeys off the suits is an important job. Without you, we'd be spending half our time reconnecting cables."

"It's not exactly the same as tracking down the hacker."

Isabelle nodded. "It's not, but it's the job for right now."

The cousins looked up as Uncle Dan bounded back into the alcove. "Are we ready to go again?"

A roar of approval came from the kids waiting. Uncle Dan called the next in line up to the tables of computers. A frazzled mom gave her two kids a small push forward.

"Okay, what book do you want to try?" Uncle

Dan asked.

A cute girl with long red hair smiled and said, "*Wind in the Willows*."

Her younger brother with the same red hair, buzzed short, crossed his arms and said, "*Peter Pan*."

"You need to pick just one," their mom said.

"We pick *Wind in the Willows*," the girl said. She looked at her brother and added, "We can ride in Mr. Toad's motorcar. You'd like that. He drives fast."

"No," the boy snapped. "We're going to fight pirates in *Peter Pan*." He glared at his sister. "You can hang around with the fairy."

"I don't want to be in a book with a bunch of smelly, wild boys," the little girl insisted.

Uncle Dan cleared his throat and looked up at Isabelle. "We can try running two books at once. We'll feed *Wind in the Willows* to one suit and *Peter Pan* to the other."

Isabelle nodded. "I can watch one. I know what to do."

The two kids beamed as Uncle Dan made the required tweaks on the computers. Soon, he sent the kids over to Carter.

"You'll need to suit them both up," Uncle Carter said. "Isabelle has to stay on the computer so we can start both books together."

"No problem," Carter said. He opened the first suit, then settled a fight over which one would climb in first by simply picking up the little girl. The little boy grumbled until Carter got him suited up as well.

The suits were soon twitching and wiggling normally. Carter went back to practicing his scary glare on the kids waiting in line. So far, none of them looked very scared. Suddenly, the lights all over the store went out.

"Oh no," a woman's voice spoke close to Carter. "A brownout." She called out to her children and must have found them because she fell silent.

"Carter," Uncle Dan said, "get the kids out of the suits."

Carter turned around carefully in the total darkness and held out his arms. His hands brushed one of the suits and he groped his way around to the back. When he tugged at the seam, nothing happened.

A thin light blinked on and Carter looked up to see Isabelle with a tiny flashlight. "I never travel without it," she said triumphantly.

"Bring it over here," Carter said. "I can't get this suit open."

"Oh, please hurry," the mother's stressed voice came from near the tables. "They must be so scared."

Isabelle pulled at the suit seam, but it held fast. "It's stuck all right," she said.

Just then, the lights came back on. "Oh, thank goodness," the mother said. "Can you get them out now?"

"Should be just a second," Uncle Dan said as the computers around him booted up again. He leaned close to the monitors. "Isabelle, can you come here, please?"

Isabelle rushed over while Carter went back to tugging on the suit seams. The suits were twitching and wiggling again, but Carter couldn't tell if it was normal suit movement or scared kid flailing.

"None of this makes any sense," Uncle Dan said.

"What do you mean?" the mother's voice rose higher. "Get my children out of those suits."

"I have the exact same stuff on my screen," Isabelle said. "Uncle Dan, I think the two books have merged. The kids are in the same program now."

Uncle Dan looked over at Carter. "I think we're going to need you again."

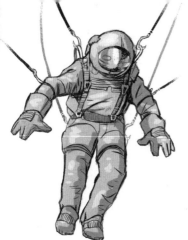

THE THIRD SUIT

"**W**hat can I do?" Carter asked.

"I need you and Isabelle to hook up that third suit," Uncle Dan said. "Then we'll patch you into the program with the kids. You can look for one of the default exits. If you bring the kids through one, the suits should open."

Carter nodded, crossing the small room quickly to drag the suit out of its box. Now that he was planning to get into the suit, he could see how ragged and patched it was. He hoped the thing was a lot safer than it looked.

Isabelle hauled a ladder back over near the other two suits. She quickly lifted the ceiling tiles out of the way and disappeared to the waist as she stood on the very top of the ladder.

50

"Okay, I have the spare cables coiled up here," she yelled down. "I'm going to drop this one and I need you to catch it."

"Sure," Carter said. He caught each cable as Isabelle dropped it. Then he tagged it with a colored sticky note so they could keep up with where it needed to connect to the third suit. The ladder trembled each time Isabelle shifted her position, but Carter held one hand on a lower rung to steady it.

The hookup went fast, almost too fast. Carter hoped Izzy had gotten all of the connections right. He didn't want to get into the suit and suddenly find he was inside a book and couldn't move . . . or breathe.

"We're set," Isabelle called down as she slipped back out of the ceiling.

Uncle Dan waved them closer so he could talk quietly. "I don't know what kind of scrambling you might find in there. I'm not sure if communication is working since the kids aren't answering. But the bail-out exits in

Wind in the Willows are at Badger's house and at Toad Hall. The bail-out exits for *Peter Pan* are on Captain Hook's ship and in Wendy's little house. Find the kids and get them out."

Carter nodded. He climbed into the suit with difficulty as the back opening was a little smaller than in the newer suits. It was a challenge for someone his height, especially since the suit dangled more than a foot off the floor. He suspected he looked silly, half falling into the suit, but no one laughed.

Isabelle closed the suit up behind him and Carter immediately noticed a sharp, unpleasant smell in the darkness. "Uh, Uncle Dan, this is the suit someone puked in it, isn't it?"

Uncle Dan didn't answer but Carter heard Isabelle laugh. Then the darkness of the suit bloomed into a misty, predawn glow. The sharp smell blended with the faintly musty smell of a slow-moving river.

Carter was standing in the middle of a small rowboat that rocked violently as he wobbled.

He looked around and the view swung so sharply that he felt his stomach roll. He sat down quickly.

"I'm in a rowboat on a river," he said. "And I can see why someone threw up in this suit."

"You'll get used to the video in a few minutes," Uncle Dan's voice said in his ear. "Are the children with you?"

Carter shook his head, then he decided not to ever do that again as another wash of nausea passed over him. He suddenly remembered that Uncle Dan couldn't see him anyway. He'd nearly made himself hurl for nothing.

"I'm alone in the boat." Then he leaned forward carefully and peered through the mist. "Wait, I see another boat. Someone's in it."

"That might be them," Uncle Dan said. "Can you reach it?"

"I can try."

Carter began rowing furiously, keeping his eyes fixed on the other boat to keep the dizziness away. He soon closed the distance between the boats. He could see two children huddled in the middle of the small, blue boat ahead of him. Slightly taller figures in what looked like fur capes sat at either end of the boat.

Carter took a deep breath to yell at the boat when he heard a weird sound. "Something's ticking," he said. "It sounds almost like an old windup alarm clock."

"Clock?" Isabelle squeaked in his ear. "That's the crocodile from *Peter Pan*. It ticks because it swallowed an alarm clock."

"There's a crocodile in here with me?" Carter shouted. "Tell me it's friendly."

"Not really," Isabelle answered. "It ate Captain Hook's hand."

"Swell," Carter mumbled. "And these are books for little kids?" He scanned the nearest bank of the river but couldn't see any sign of a crocodile. The far bank was invisible in the mist.

Then he heard a shriek from the boat ahead. Carter's head snapped up. He saw the crocodile break through the water at the side of the ship. The ticking grew louder as the huge animal opened its jaws wide.

Both the children and the hooded figures panicked and scrambled away from the crocodile's jaws. Just as Carter reached them, the boat tipped. Its riders were dumped into the river. Before the crocodile could vanish, Carter quickly shoved one of his oars into its open mouth.

The huge creature strained for a moment then snapped its jaws shut, turning Carter's oar into splinters of wood.

"Whoa," Carter yelped. "That thing has some bite."

"Crocodiles have huge bite force!" Isabelle shouted in his ear. "But the muscles opening their mouths are weak. You can hold its jaws shut!"

Carter didn't like the idea of getting his hands that close to the crocodile. The huge creature turned in the water and smacked its head into the side of Carter's rowboat, making it tilt dangerously. Carter threw his weight to one side to tilt the boat back away from the water. The boat quickly resettled.

Carter pulled off his T-shirt. When the crocodile rose out of the water, he slipped the shirt over its jaw and twisted it tightly. The crocodile jerked backward immediately, thrashing in an effort to get free. Its huge tail flailed until it smacked the side of the rowboat, knocking a hole through the wood.

The boat sank in seconds, and Carter swam away from the thrashing crocodile. He scanned the water for the kids and spotted their heads near the far bank. One of the mysterious figures from the boat was towing the children and the other figure.

Carter felt a surge of relief. At least the kids hadn't drowned. Carter began to swim for the shore. He just hoped he could reach the kids before they ended up in any more trouble.

THE LOST BOYS

By the time Carter reached the shore, the kids were nowhere to be seen. He wiped his dripping hair out of his eyes and looked around. He stood at the edge of thick woods where the darkness was complete. Carter couldn't imagine two little kids wandering in such spooky woods.

"I'm facing thick woods," he said. "Would that be *Peter Pan* or *Wind in the Willows*?"

"Hard to say for sure," Isabelle said. "If it's *Wind in the Willows*, then Badger lives in there."

"And there's an exit at his house," Carter said.

"Should be," Uncle Dan agreed.

Carter took a deep breath to yell the kids' names, then realized he didn't know them. He asked and waited a moment before Uncle Dan said, "Colin and Emmy."

"Thanks." Carter stepped into the woods and walked forward carefully, calling for the kids. Only the soft rustle of the woods answered. Then Carter began to see faces peering out at him from the brambles and underbrush.

He wasn't able to see them when he peered directly into a mass of undergrowth. As soon as he began to turn away, he caught sight of what looked like a face.

"Is anyone there?" Carter called out. "I'm looking for two little kids."

The woods just rustled around him. As he walked, he caught sight of more faces from the corner of his eye. He got the sense that they didn't like him to be in the woods.

"They're probably just scared," he muttered.

Then he heard running feet. He stopped, trying to decide what direction the sound came from. The footsteps were padded but sounded like many creatures.

Suddenly, something burst from the

underbrush and dashed by him. It was a rabbit. "Get out while you can," the rabbit gasped as it galloped past. "Get out!"

"Why?" Carter yelled. "I'm looking for two kids!" But the rabbit just dashed back into the rough undergrowth. Carter shuddered. "I'm starting to get a serious rabbit phobia."

"Really?" Izzy's voice sounded amused. "Rabbits?"

"I didn't ask you," Carter snapped. The sound of running feet grew louder. Carter picked up his pace, breaking into a light jog. He knew better than to run in the woods where roots and exposed rocks could trip him easily.

Finally he broke into a small clearing. In the center, two fallen trees had crashed together, forming a kind of wild shelter. A small head covered with red curls poked up above one of the rocks.

"Duck!" she yelled.

Carter knew enough about these books to hit the ground immediately. Arrows sailed over his head, swishing through the space his body had occupied just moments before.

"Arrows?" he said.

"That'd be the lost boys," Izzy said.

"Great." Carter began to crawl toward the fallen trees as more arrows swished through the air. He ducked under one of the wedged tree trunks. The rough bark of the tree scraped against his bare back and he wished he hadn't lost his T-shirt.

"What are you doing here?" Emmy asked. "I thought this was our turn."

"It is, but haven't you noticed things have gotten a little rough in this book?" he asked.

"Yeah," her brother said from his spot in the small, protected space. "It's fantastic!"

"Hullo," said the small figure wedged in the crook of the tree.

Carter realized then that the hooded figures weren't hooded at all. They were furry. One was a water rat and the other a mole, who peered fretfully at Carter.

"You're a big one," the mole said. "Are you nice?"

"I try," Carter said. "Right now, I have to get Emmy and Colin out of here."

"That might be difficult," Rat said. "What with the arrows and all. It's quite unusual for the weasels to use arrows. They're usually fonder of bashing with clubs and punching."

"They aren't weasels," Colin said, his voice high with excitement. "They're lost boys."

"Oh," Ratty said. "Perhaps they simply need us to find them."

"No," Colin said firmly. "They don't want to be found. They want a mother."

"A mother?" Carter said. "Where do we get one of those."

"Emmy could do it," Colin said.

"No, I could not," Emmy snapped. "Mom read us that book and being the mother means work, work, work. Wendy might think that sounds like fun, but I do not."

"Maybe you could pretend," Carter said,

ducking as arrows thunked into the tree trunks. "Just so we can get out of here alive."

"Okay," Emmy grumbled. She raised her voice and yelled, "Hey boys, I will be your mother if you want!"

The rain of arrows stopped. A voice called out. "Really? Are you nice?"

"Not so much," Colin muttered. His sister poked him in the ribs until he yelped.

"I'm very nice," she shouted. "And I just love to sew and wash clothes and cook."

Carter rolled his eyes. She was laying it on too thick. The boys would surely be able to tell she was lying.

"Okay, come out and be our mother," the boy's voice called.

Emmy started to crawl over the nearest fallen tree, but Carter pulled her back. "I'll go first," he said. "Just to be sure it's safe."

"But I'm the one they want," she said.

"Tough." Carter yelled out into the woods, "I'm coming out first. If you shoot me, your mother won't come out to see you."

"We won't shoot you."

Carter wasn't sure how much he believed the voice, but he certainly couldn't get the kids out of this mess by hiding forever in the pile of trees. He scrambled over the tree trunk, holding his breath and hoping no one shot him.

When he stood in the open for a moment, a small group of ragged boys slipped out of their hiding places in the woods. The boys seemed to all be about Colin's age.

"Where's our mother?" one dirty child demanded.

"Right here."

Carter spun around to see Emmy scrambling over the fallen tree. She marched over until she stood beside Carter.

"Shame on you for shooting at us!" she said.

"We thought you might be pirates," one of the boys said sheepishly.

As they talked, Colin scrambled out too, grinning at the boys. "Hallo, guys," he said.

"Hallo, Colin," they called back. "We thought we lost you in the great darkness."

"I thought so, too," Colin said. "Everything was scrambled. Where's Peter?"

The boys shrugged in unison. "We haven't seen him since the darkness."

"We'll find Peter," another boy called. "Come on, Colin. Come on, Mother."

"Oh no," Carter said, grabbing Colin and Emmy. "We have to head to Badger's house."

Instantly every boy notched an arrow and pointed it at Carter. "You best let our friend and our mother go," one boy said. "Or we'll kill you dead."

"Kill me?" Carter yelped. "What kind of kids' book is this?"

"Be careful," Uncle Dan said in his ear. "The lost boys were fairly good at killing things."

"Of course they are," Carter said, stepping away slowly, still dragging the two red-headed children with him. He looked from arrow to arrow. Now what was he supposed to do?

THE MERMAIDS' LAGOON

For a moment, no one spoke. Carter eased backward toward the tree line, and the boys held their arrows up, aimed directly at him. Then, everyone froze. From the trail, they heard the sound of a clock ticking.

"Crocodile!" the boys shouted. They slung their bows over their shoulders and raced for the woods.

"Crocodile?" Colin said. "Cool!"

"It's not cool," his sister snapped, then she squirmed around and glared at Carter. "What are you going to do to keep us safe?"

Carter pushed the kids behind him and picked up one of the stray branches from the fallen tree. "Just stay behind me."

The ticktock of the crocodile grew louder. Carter's knees shook, but he stood his ground. He held the branch like a baseball bat, ready to hit a homer as soon as the crocodile appeared.

They heard a rustle just beyond the path and the ticking rang still louder. Then a furry brown shape broke from the path and into the clearing. It was Mr. Rat!

"Ticktock, everyone!" he said.

"That was you?" Carter sputtered.

"Those boys didn't seem interested in the likes of Mole and I, so we slipped off into the tree line and made like a crocodile!"

Colin and Emmy raced toward the rat and threw themselves on him in a hug. "Well now!" Rat said, looking totally embarrassed.

"You're the best!" Colin said.

Mr. Mole stepped nervously into the clearing then. Emmy gave him a hug as well. "Thanks for helping out," she said.

Mole looked as pleased as someone with a

thickly furred face and almost no eyes can. "It really was all Ratty's idea," he said modestly.

"Thanks for that," Carter said. "Now can you help us find Badger's house?"

Rat looked at Carter sharply, his ears sharply at attention and his nose twitching nervously. "Oh no, he wouldn't like that at all. He's very shy. He's sure to be offended. That's quite out of the question."

"It's where we have to go," Carter insisted. "If you're afraid, maybe you could just point us in the right direction."

"I'm not afraid," Rat said.

"Ratty's quite brave," Mole said in support of his friend.

"But I've never called on him at his own home myself," Rat said. "And I know him so well. Besides, he lives in the very middle of the Wild Wood."

"Is that where we are?" Carter asked. "The Wild Wood?"

Rat nodded. "Though not nearly the center.

It's a long way to the center."

"Which direction?" Carter asked.

Rat sighed and pointed in the direction the lost boys had vanished.

Of course, Carter thought gloomily. "That's the way we have to go. Thanks."

Carter turned and herded Colin and Emmy toward the tree line.

"Wait," called Mole. "I'll come with you. I've been wanting to visit with Badger."

"Oh, I'll come as well. It won't do to let Mole go without me," Rat said. "There are a hundred things one has to know, which we understand all about and you don't. I mean passwords, signs, and sayings that have power and effect. They are all simple enough when you know them, but they've got to be known if you're small. Or you'll find yourself in trouble."

"Thank you," Mole said quietly.

"The worst of it is, I don't exactly know where we are," Rat said. "Those wild children chased us for a bit. And we were in rather a hurry when we began after our run-in with that ticking toothy beast."

"Nothing's ever easy," Carter said.

"The best adventures aren't," Mole agreed cheerfully.

Rat picked up another broken branch to carry as a club. Colin quickly followed his example. Armed as well as they were likely to be, they walked into the shadowy woods and began the search for Badger's house.

For a while, they walked quietly, since walking on the uneven ground took all their attention. The roots and rocks seemed to try harder to trip them than ever. Also, they had to change the order in which they walked several times.

Rat led the way, but Emmy walked so quickly that she stayed directly behind the giant rat. At close range, the smell of wet rat fur made her sneeze.

"You smell like a wet dog," she complained.

Rat drew himself up, deeply insulted. "I

most certainly do not smell like any sort of dog. I smell like a wet rat."

"Which smells worse than a dog," Emmy complained.

Carter hurried to separate the two before Rat smacked her with his club. Carter dragged her back until she was behind Colin. That worked for a few minutes, until it became obvious that Colin was carefully bending back branches as he walked. Then, he was letting them go at exactly the right moment to smack Emmy in the face.

Carter reached them as Emmy picked up a rock to throw at Colin. He disarmed her and sent Colin up to walk behind Rat and in front of Mole. Thankfully, Colin didn't seem to mind the smell of either creature. They soon ended up walking three across, whispering as they went.

This made Carter nervous. He wondered what Colin might be plotting.

"Rescuing these kids would be easier if they wanted to be rescued," he muttered.

"Haven't you ever babysat?" Isabelle's voice spoke so suddenly in Carter's ear that he actually turned around to look for her.

"No," he said. "I mowed lawns."

"Well, there are certain rules to little kids," Isabelle said. "Brothers and sisters don't get along until they're grown. And if they figure out how to make the babysitter's life miserable, they probably will."

"Swell," Carter said. "But I'm not babysitting. I'm not their babysitter. I'm the hero."

"Do you always talk to yourself?" Emmy asked as she stomped along beside him.

"I'm not talking to myself," he said, "I'm talking to my cousin. She's helping run the program we're in."

"Oh," Emmy said. "Why doesn't she talk to me?"

"We think the electrical problems messed up communication with your suit."

"Is that why it went dark for a while?" she asked. "That was cool."

Carter looked at her in surprise. "You weren't scared?"

It was her turn to looked surprised. "Why would I be?"

Carter didn't have an answer to that. He heard sounds of surprise from Colin and his furry pals, so he trotted to catch up. They had broken through the trees and into another clearing.

This one was filled with a large lagoon. Carter could see what looked like a slow river flowing into it. A faint mist rose from the lagoon, even though the sun shone on it brightly. Even from where they stood, Carter could smell the faint scent of salt water.

A saltwater lagoon in the middle of the woods was strange enough to bring gasps from the group. But it was the mermaids perched on rocks around the lagoon that surprised Carter the most.

"Mermaids?" Carter said.

"The mermaid lagoon?" Isabelle asked in his

ear. "That's from *Peter Pan*."

"They don't drown people or anything fun like that do they?" Carter asked.

"No," Isabelle said. "They mostly play catch with bubbles and comb their hair."

"Okay," Carter said. "I can deal with that."

He walked up to Rat and Mole, who were staring at the mermaids.

"I've been in the Wild Woods many times," Rat said, "and I have never seen this."

"I think it's new," Carter said.

"Can we sit down for a while?" Emmy asked. "I'm tired."

"I guess that would be okay," Carter said. "I need to figure out how to get around this."

Emmy and Colin ran to the edge of the lagoon. At the sight of them, the mermaids quickly dove into the water and disappeared. "Oh, that's no fun," Emmy complained.

The children hopped from rock to rock.

"Hey, be careful!" Carter yelled. Naturally, the children ignored him.

They kept hopping until they reached a huge rock near the center of the lagoon. They flopped down on it and scooted near the edge to peer into the water. With a sigh, Carter began stepping carefully on the rocks to reach them.

The warm sunshine felt good as he walked, drying the last bit of damp from his clothes. But when he reached the large rock, the sky went dark suddenly. Carter looked up in surprise at the dark clouds. The lagoon grew so dim, it was difficult to see.

"Maybe we should go back," he said nervously. That's when he heard a rhythmic splashing in the water. He knew the sound. It was oars.

"I hear oars," he said.

"Pirates!" Isabelle warned. "Get off the rock!"

Carter turned and waved at Rat and Mole, signaling them to hide. Then he leaned down and whispered to Colin and Emmy. "Dive!"

SAVE THE GIRL

Without another word, both kids jumped into the water. Carter watched to see that Emmy and Colin popped quickly to the surface near the rock. Then he dove in as well and gently coaxed the kids to cling to a hidden cleft in the rock.

The sound of oars grew louder. Carter eased around the rock to a place where he could see without being seen. He spotted the small boat and three figures heading toward them. Two of the figures were dressed much like the pirate crew he remembered from his time in *Treasure Island*.

The third person in the boat was a girl about Carter's age. As they grew closer, Carter saw she had big, brown eyes and long, straight, black hair. She was also tied up. Carter frowned. Rescuing book characters wasn't really part of his job, but he couldn't just leave them to hurt her.

Apparently, the pirates couldn't see quite as clearly as Carter. They plowed their boat right into the side of the rock where Carter and the kids clung.

"Stuckey, you lubber," one pirate called sharply, "here's the rock. Now help me get the girl on the rock before the tide comes in."

The two men wrestled the girl onto the rock. She sat stiffly and neither helped nor fought them.

"Well, Smee," the other pirate said, "don't she look nice there? It almost makes me sad to think of her drowning when the tide comes in."

Both men laughed at this and sat back into their boat, rowing sharply away.

Carter watched the boat ease away from the rock and relaxed. He would simply wait until they were gone, and then he'd untie the girl.

"Boat ahoy!" a rough voice rolled across the lagoon.

"The captain," Smee said.

"Boat ahoy!"

The sound of splashing came just before Carter spotted a dark figure swimming quickly toward the small boat. A hook rose up out of the water and snagged the side of the boat. Then the pirate captain climbed quickly into it.

"Captain, is all well?" Stuckey asked.

Hook sighed. "The boys are looking for a mother." His eyes flashed to the shore. "They found one in these cursed woods, then lost her again. But they'll find her again, I fear, and she'll keep them safe."

"That would be bad," Smee agreed. "What if we find the mother and keep her for our own?"

"Ah, there's a scheme," Hook said cheerfully. "We'll act on it as soon as I watch Tiger Lily drown."

Carter frowned. If the pirates didn't leave, he couldn't save the girl. And he really wanted to save the girl. Suddenly he had an idea.

"Ticktock," he called out, imitating the sound of the crocodile just as Rat had. "Ticktock."

Carter could see the fear pass over the pirates' faces. "To the ship!" Hook cried. "Get me away from that evil creature."

Smee and Stuckey began to row away while Hook bellowed at them to move faster. When Carter couldn't see them anymore, he scrambled up onto the rock beside the girl. Then he pulled the kids out of the water.

"Help me untie her," Carter said. "We need to hurry, in case they come back."

The dark-haired girl looked sharply at him. "Who are you? I do not know you."

"I'm Carter," he said. "I'm just visiting."

"I thank you, Carter. I am Tiger Lily."

Carter recognized the knots the pirates had used from his two years in Boy Scouts. He was able to untie them quickly. Finally, they all scrambled from the rock to the shore. This meant more than a little splashing, since several of the rocks they had used to cross earlier were now underwater.

On the shore, the girl turned to Carter and said, "I must now return to my people. Again, I thank you, Carter."

"I'm glad to help," Carter said. Then Emmy stepped on his foot and looked up at him fiercely. "Um, I'm glad we could *all* help."

Tiger Lily looked down at Emmy. "Are you the mother the pirates mentioned?"

"No!" she snapped. "I do not want to be the mother of a bunch of grubby boys!"

"Hey, you aren't all that clean either," Colin said.

Emmy just sniffed.

"I don't suppose you know where Badger's house is?" Carter asked.

Tiger Lily shook her head. "I do not know Badger."

Carter sighed. "I figured."

Tiger Lily smiled at the children, then she nodded to Carter before she slipped away into the brush. Just as she vanished, Rat and Mole popped out from behind a tree.

"Were those real pirates?" Mole asked. "How exciting!"

"I don't like to think of pirates on the river," Rat said. Then he sniffed and shook his head. "That doesn't smell like the river."

"I think it's a lagoon," Carter said. "From the ocean."

"Lad," Rat said, shaking his head, "the sea is nowhere near here."

"I think it is now," Carter said.

Rat sniffed again and just shook his head again. "Strange happenings, even for the Wild Wood."

"Okay, do you have any idea how to get to Badger's house from here?" Carter asked.

Rat sighed. "We need to get to the other side of this bit of water. I might find my way then."

"Okay, then we circle the lagoon," Carter announced. "Staying in the woods so we don't run into pirates."

80

"Carter," Uncle Dan's voice spoke in Carter's ear, "I've got a very upset mother here."

"Tell her the kids are having a great time," Carter answered. "But I'm still looking for Badger's house. I'm open to suggestions if you have any."

"I have one," Emmy said. "Why not just open the suits and let us climb out?"

Carter sighed. "I tried that. They're stuck. But we think they'll open when we find an exit. There's one at Badger's house."

The group trudged back into the woods. They walked in silence, keeping the sound of the lagoon on their left so they knew they must be circling the lagoon.

Finally they saw the trees were thinning and the shadows of the woods brightened as more light poured in. Rat stopped and cocked his head, looking around.

"We should be getting deeper in the Wild Wood," he said. "This doesn't make sense."

Carter felt sorry for the big rat. Clearly the

scrambling of the books was very confusing for the characters trying to work within it.

"Well, maybe we should just keep going," Carter suggested. "Let's walk away from the lagoon. Maybe that will help."

The group turned so the lagoon sounds were at their backs. Then they marched forward. The woods around them grew brighter and brighter. Clearly they were not getting deeper into the Wild Wood.

Finally, they broke through the tree line and were facing a wide, hard-packed dirt road. They stepped into the road, looking up and down it.

"What's this road doing here?" Ratty demanded, stomping his foot and raising a small puff of dust.

"Someone's coming," Emmy said. "I hear them."

"Everyone out of the road," Carter said as he heard the chug of an engine and the wild honking of a horn. An antique car sailed over the hill, forcing them to jump the last few feet out of the road as it zoomed past. Dirt flew behind it, sending them all into coughing fits. Even with the haze of dirt, Carter could see the car held two well-dressed young men and a toad in a dress. The toad was driving.

"Toad!" Rat screamed at the car.

"Oh, Mr. Toad is driving again," Mole said. "How wonderful."

"It isn't wonderful," Rat said sharply. "He's wild as a young goat."

Carter let out a yelp. "We need to follow him. There's an exit at Toad Hall."

"Oh my," Rat said unhappily as Carter dashed down the road.

The group raced after Carter. The kids were soon close behind him. Rat could have probably kept up with the kids, but he clearly slowed down to run beside his friend. Mole's running looked more like a lively waddle.

Soon, they all reached the top of the next hill. Looking down the other side, they saw the car had plowed through a thick holly hedge and ended up in a muddy pond. Toad was limping around the edge of the pond, picking prickles out of his nose. He wore a tattered dress and a black bonnet that half covered one eye. Behind him in the pond, the two young men sat in the car, holding their heads and moaning slightly.

"Toad, what are you up to?" Rat demanded.

"Did you see me?" Toad asked, his eyes wide. "I am the Toad, the motor-car snatcher, the prison-breaker, the Toad who always escapes!"

"Then we'd best escape before those gentlemen feel better," Rat said, pointing to the young men who had tumbled out of the car and were wading slowly toward shore.

"We should go to your house," Carter said.

Rat twitched his nose. "That could be a problem," he said solemnly.

TOAD HALL

Carter and Toad turned to look at Rat. Together they said, "Why is that a problem?"

Rat looked in surprise at Toad. "You mean you haven't heard?"

"Heard what?" asked Toad, turning rather pale. "Go on, Ratty! Quick! Don't spare me! What haven't I heard?"

"Do you mean to tell me," shouted Rat, shaking his shaggy head at his friend, "that you've heard nothing about the Stoats and Weasels?"

"What, the Wild Wooders?" cried Toad, trembling in every limb. "No, not a word! What have they been doing?"

"—And how they've taken Toad Hall?" continued Rat.

Toad began to moan and large tears dripped

down his face. Carter looked between the two animals. "Is that going to be a problem?"

"A problem?" Rat said in a squeak. "Only if you want to keep your head on your shoulders."

"It was horrible," Mole said. "Badger and I were at the hall when they came. We were guarding it because the Wild Wooders had already talked about taking over since you were gone for so long, Toad."

"I was having adventures!" Toad insisted.

"It happened at night," Rat added when Mole fell silent with a shudder. "A *very* dark night, raining and blowing hard, too. A band of armed weasels crept silently up to the front entrance. At the same time, a body of desperate ferrets took over the backyard. And a company of skirmishing stoats snuck into the conservatory and the billiard room."

"Badger and I were sitting by the fire telling stories," Mole said in a whisper. "Those bloodthirsty villains broke down the doors and rushed in upon us. We fought and Badger was brilliant, but we were taken by surprise. They turned us out into the cold and the wet with many insulting and uncalled-for remarks!"

Toad snickered a bit at that, until Rat said, "They've been there ever since, Toad."

"They have?" Toad said, bending down to snatch up a stick. "We'll see about that!" Then he spun and marched down the road.

"It's no good, Toad," Mole shouted. "There's at least a hundred of them."

Toad never even looked back. Carter didn't know how they were going to get into Toad Hall, but he knew there was an exit there.

"Let's go," he said as he trotted after Toad.

"You'll get yourself killed!" Rat shouted as the two children happily followed Carter.

Finally, Rat and Mole moaned. Then they followed the children. The group made an odd parade down the road with no one talking. Colin bent down and scooped up a small rock now and then, cramming them in his pockets.

As they approached the house, Rat finally ran

up and caught at Toad's sleeve. "What do you intend to do?"

"Tell them to get out of my house!" Toad said.

"They have sentries," Rat said. "They'll not turn the house over just because you ask."

"What if we came by the river in that boat of yours?"

"First, a crocodile ate my boat," Rat said. "Second, they have stoats watching the bridge."

As they stared at the huge house, Carter began to feel a little desperate. An exit from the program lay just ahead. All they had to do was get in. Suddenly, they all jumped at a rustling in the bushes. Out popped a large furry creature.

"Badger!" Mole cried. "We found Toad."

"So I see," Badger said. "And what do you propose to do now, Toad?"

"Get back my home," Toad said bravely. "I know you all think I'm silly, but this is my home and I'll not hand it over to those creatures!"

"Don't be in such a rush," Badger said. "I know a secret. There is an underground passage that leads from the riverbank some distance from here, right up into the middle of Toad Hall."

"That's fantastic," Carter said.

Badger peered at Carter and the children. "And who are you?"

Introductions and explanations were quickly made. Badger seemed doubtful about the talk of pirates and crocodiles and lagoons in the middle of the Wild Wood, but he was polite enough.

When they finished their tale, it was Toad who interrupted. "Oh, nonsense! I know every inch of Toad Hall, inside and out. There are no tunnels or magic exits, I do assure you!"

"Your father told me of the passage," Badger said. "He felt it better not to tell you. He thought you might have trouble keeping the secret."

Toad grumbled a bit at this, but finally cheered up. "I am a bit of a talker."

"At any rate, I have found out they are having a party in a few hours," Badger said. "They'll pull all the guards except the sentries. By then, we can be in place and storm the hall."

"Hours?" Colin grumbled. "But I'm hungry."

"And tired," Emmy added.

Carter leaned over and whispered. "Time can fold up a bit in the program. I'll get you out as quick as I can."

"Then we'd best head for the river straight away," Badger said.

The group trooped down to the riverbank. Badger led them along the river for a little way. Suddenly, he swung himself over the edge into a hole in the riverbank, a little above the water. Mole and Rat followed silently, swinging themselves into the hole. Carter handed down each of the children, then he followed.

When it came to Toad's turn, he slipped and fell into the water with a loud splash and a squeal of alarm. Carter had the longest arms, so he leaned far out of the hole and hauled Toad in.

The secret tunnel was cold, dark, damp, low, and narrow. Badger had a lantern, but the way was so narrow that they had to walk single file.

Carter noticed Toad shivering. He suspected it was partly from fear and partly because he was wet.

Toad began to lag behind the group a little in the darkness. Colin walked just ahead of Carter but he kept glancing back at Toad. Finally he slipped behind Carter. Under his breath, the little boy said, "Ticktock. Ticktock."

Toad yelped, clearly remembering the crocodile. He rushed past Colin, nearly knocking the little boy down. Then he ducked and skidded right between Carter's legs and just kept going. He squished past Emmy and ran right into Rat. This pushed Rat into Mole and Mole into Badger.

Badger thought they were being attacked from behind! He struggled to decide what weapon could work in the tight tunnel. When he realized Toad had plowed into him, he said, "I say that tiresome Toad *shall* be left behind!"

"It wasn't totally Toad's fault," Carter said from the back of the line, where he held Colin by the arm. "Colin was playing crocodile."

"Do you see?" Toad said. "It wasn't my fault."

"Not totally," Carter said.

Badger finally nodded. "All right, but no more games. This is serious business."

Carter gave the little boy a look, and the boy nodded quickly. Carter smiled. *I must finally be getting the hang of "the look,"* he thought.

They shuffled along a bit farther and Badger whispered, "We ought to be nearly under the hall."

Soon, they could hear muffled voices coming from above. By the sound of it, there were a lot of voices. The passage began to slope upward and the voices grew louder. Now with the voices, they heard the stamping of feet and the clinking of glasses and dishes.

They hurried along the passage till it came to a full stop. There, they found themselves standing under a trapdoor.

"That leads to the butler's pantry, so we should be able to make our entrance unnoticed," Badger said.

The party was so loud, it completely covered any noise they might make. They heaved open the trapdoor and scrambled out into the pantry.

Carter opened the door a crack and looked out. What he saw made him draw a sharp breath. The room was filled with creatures as he expected, but they had guests. Hook's pirates milled through the crowd! Captain Hook himself stood at the head of a great table next to the biggest weasel Carter had ever seen.

"Oh great," he said, "the pirates and the weasels are pals."

"Pirates?" Toad squealed in great excitement. He crowded against the door next to Carter, moving so quickly that Carter couldn't catch the door against the increased weight. The door swung open with a bang, and Carter fell to the floor with Toad sprawled on top if him. Every eye in the hall turned toward them.

"Intruders!" bellowed Captain Hook and the Chief Weasel together. "Get them!"

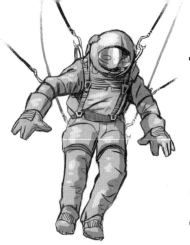

THE GRAND BATTLE

Carter struggled to heave Toad off, but the closest weasels tugged him off instead. Then two pirates hauled Carter to his feet. He managed a quick glance into the butler's pantry but saw no sign of Badger, Rat, Mole, or the children.

The weasels quickly tied Toad up in gold cords pulled from the drapes. They wrapped them around and around Toad as he shouted insults at them. Then, they hung him on a hook on the wall where he wriggled and blustered.

"Ah, nice of our host to drop in," the Chief Weasel shouted. "Good Toad, Honest Toad, Modest Toad." At each compliment the crowd roared with laughter.

Toad continued to rant until one of the weasels

snatched a pumpkin from the table and stuffed it in his mouth.

"That'll suit you nicely," the weasel said.

"Well," Captain Hook said, striding over to poke Carter with his hook, "and who is this?"

Carter simply glared without answering.

"Must be some friend of Toad's," the Chief Weasel said.

"He mustn't know Toad very well," someone shouted and another hail of laughter rang out.

"Well," Captain Hook said, "Mr. Toad makes a fine mascot for the wall, but I see no use in this one. Unless you'd like to join my crew. You look able enough."

"No," Carter said. "I passed on joining Long John Silver and I'll pass on joining you."

"I don't know this Silver," Hook said. "But if you'll not join us, I see no reason to leave you alive."

"Make him walk the plank," Smee shouted.

"You might notice," Hook said dryly, "that we don't have a plank handy or a ship either."

"We could make him walk off the table," one of the weasels suggested.

Hook just looked at him. "It wouldn't have quite the same feeling without the sea full of sharks."

The weasel seemed to think about that a moment. "We could get some little dogs to nip at him when he hits the floor."

Hook shook his head. "Not the same."

The weasel looked quite disappointed at that. Silence fell over the room while everyone thought about the best way to put an end to Carter.

"What if we tossed him off the roof?" another weasel suggested. "Into a holly hedge. Holly has teeth!"

Hook seemed to give this some thought. "Okay, it's not as good as a good walk off the plank, but it could work."

"What if we put a door on the edge of the roof," the Chief Weasel said. "That would be like a plank."

Hook nodded. "It'll have to do."

The weasels quickly set to yanking on the nearest door, the one to the butler's pantry. When it didn't pull free, a couple began bashing it with their clubs.

"Hey, there," the Chief Weasel called out. "That won't help anything."

"This isn't working," one of the weasels complained. "Let's just hit him instead."

"That'll work," the Chief Weasel said. "I'm tired of all this anyway. I want to eat."

So the weasels turned and rushed at Carter. Although he doubted the program would actually let him be bashed to death by clubs, he didn't look forward to just how much the next few minutes might hurt.

Just as the weasels reached him, something crashed through the tall windows near the table. The shower of glass drove several of the closest weasels to dive under the table.

"What's up now?" the Chief Weasel said.

A boy leaped through the window and landed

on the table. He was about Emmy's age, Carter guessed, and wore clothes that looked to be made from leaves stuck together with tree sap. When he grinned at the stunned faces surrounding him, Carter noticed his teeth were very small and white.

"Peter Pan?" Carter guessed.

"Do I know you?" Peter asked, peering at Carter. "Michael? John?"

"Carter."

"I thought so," Peter said. "You're too tall for Michael or John. You're not a pirate, are you?"

"No," Carter said. "I'm a captive."

"Then let's have a battle!" he crowed.

Instantly a volley of arrows came flying through the broken window. All of the weasels who weren't already under the table tried to crowd in. The pirates tried too, but the weasels quickly shoved them back out.

The only pirate not scrambling for a hiding place was Hook. He strode toward the table, drawing his sword as he went.

"So, Pan," the pirate said, "this is all your doing."

"Ay, James Hook," came the stern answer, "it is all my doing."

"Prepare to meet thy doom," said Hook.

As the two set at one another with swords, the lost boys began to scramble through the window. At the same time, Badger, Rat, Mole, and the children came pouring out of the butler's pantry while howling and swinging clubs.

The pirates and weasels not under the table were pinned between the two groups. At first, Carter wondered if he should pull the kids out of the fight. Then he saw Colin swing a club at a weasel, making it jump back. The jump made the weasel fall backward over Emmy, who had crouched on the floor behind it. Carter grinned. The kids made a pretty good team.

Carter knew the best thing to do would be to grab the kids and search for the exit, but he decided he could rescue Toad first. Poor Toad looked miserable as he hung squirming and watching the battle going on without him.

Carter strode across the room and lifted Toad from the hook on the wall. Toad blinked at him gratefully. Carter looked at the pumpkin, unsure of how to best pry it out of the Toad's mouth.

As he bent over to look closely at the pumpkin, something slammed him in the back, driving him forward. He smacked into Toad's belly with such force that the pumpkin was immediately ejected. It flew across the room.

Carter scrambled up from the floor to face the grinning pirate who had kicked him into Toad. The pirate raised his sword and took a wild swing toward Carter. Carter ducked. Toad squealed as the tip of the sword raked across his middle, slicing cleanly through the ropes. The ropes fell in a pile on the floor.

The pirate bent over, clearly intending to hack into Carter with his sword. At that moment, Emmy and Colin each brought a thick branch down hard on the pirate's head. The man collapsed in a pile.

Carter scrambled up. "Um, be sure you never

do that to a real person."

"Please," Emmy said, "we know that."

"We're not babies," Colin said.

"Okay, okay," Carter held up his hands. "I just don't want your mom yelling at my uncle if you guys go home and bash the neighbor."

"We would never do that," Emmy said. "Our neighbor is about a million years old."

"And she gives us cookies!" Colin added with a grin.

"Okay, good," Carter said. "Now we need to look for the program exit."

"What does it look like?" Colin asked.

"It's usually marked with an x," Carter said.

Toad tugged on his clothes and pointed. "Like that?"

Carter turned and looked across the room. The pumpkin had splattered when Toad coughed it out. Now it ran slowly down the opposite wall, leaving a long jagged X in golden pumpkin pulp.

Carter grinned. "Yep, exactly like that."

X MARKS THE SPOT

Finally, Carter had found an exit from this crazy adventure.

All they had to do was cross a room filled with battling weasels and pirates with swords to reach it. Carter took a deep breath. "Let's do it."

Emmy and Colin gave him a quick grin and dashed into the crowd. Carter quickly saw that being smaller gave them a huge advantage.

Emmy dropped to her knees and skidded on the smooth wood floor, sliding right between the bowed legs of one pirate as he clashed swords with one of the lost boys. The pirate was so startled by the girl, that he fell over onto his back.

Colin darted and slid as quickly as his sister, pausing only now and then to add his own mayhem to the fight. He slipped under a table and tied the boot laces of a weasel together, sending the animal crashing when it lunged after Mole.

Carter's trip through the crowd was harder. He took up a lot more room and every time he passed one of the weasels or pirates, he found himself in a new fight. He scooped a fallen sword off the floor and jumped onto the long dining room table to get out of the thickest part of the crowd.

He had to jump from the table halfway down, as Peter stood on the table to give him the advantage over Hook. As Carter slipped around the tall pirate, Hook ran into him and his sword clattered to the floor. Hook turned to snarl at Carter, and Peter took advantage of his distraction to slice off a lock of Hook's long hair. Hook roared and turned back to his fight with the boy.

Carter bent to grab the sword, but one of the weasels kicked it away and swung a heavy club at Carter's head. Carter ducked, just avoiding a heavy knock on the head. Suddenly Emmy and Colin appeared behind the weasel and grabbed its pants, dragging them to the floor.

The weasel squeaked in alarm and fumbled to pull its pants back up. Carter simply ducked around it and hustled the kids toward the wall.

Then they heard a howling cry and saw three of the weasels had crawled from under the table and were running at them, clubs held high. Carter looked around for a weapon, but the little boy behind him simply dug into his pockets, pulling out handfuls of small rocks. Colin threw the rocks on the floor under the weasel's feet. The creatures slipped and skidded on the rolling pebbles and bashed into one another, ending up in a pile on the floor.

"Nice job, kid," Carter said.

They only had to hop over one sprawled pirate and duck under two weasels throwing fruit to finally reach the wall.

Carter leaned against the X, gasping. He ran his hands up and down the wall, looking for a doorknob or some obvious way to open it.

"This is supposed to be a door?" Emmy asked.

"Yeah," Carter said. "We just have to figure out how to open it."

Finally Colin said, "I found a hole in the wall. Does that mean anything?"

Carter ran his hand over the hole. It was hidden in a knothole in the wood paneling on the lower half of the wall. The hole was perfectly round and smooth. He looked around for something to shove into the hole. He spotted the stem of the pumpkin laying at his feet. He picked it up and rammed it, skinny end first, into the hole.

The fatter part of the stem made a perfect doorknob, though a bit sticky. Carter turned it and the door opened. Beyond it they saw nothing but a brightly lit tunnel.

"This is our way home," he told the kids.

Colin looked back at the room. "I hate to leave before the good guys win," he said. "They might need us."

"They'll be okay," Emmy told him, patting his

arm. "The good guys win. They always win in the best books."

Colin nodded. "Bye everyone!" he shouted.

For an instant, the fighting stopped and everyone turned to the sound of the boy's voice. Peter Pan raised his sword in salute. The lost boys cheered, and the weasels hooted. One or two pirates even waved a little, until Hook gave them the evil eye.

Badger called out, "Good traveling!"

"Come back again," Mr. Toad said.

"We'll try," Emmy shouted back.

Carter just smiled and nodded, urging the kids through the door. They stepped into the near-blinding light of the tunnel. The door swung shut behind them with a soft click. Then the lights went out.

Carter was immediately aware of the closeness of his suit and the sharp smell of old vomit. "I'm not getting into this suit again until it's cleaned," he muttered.

"It's been cleaned," Uncle Dan's voice said in

his ear. "Several times."

Carter tried not to fidget as he waited for the seam to open behind him. He knew they would want to get the children out of the suits first. Though it was probably only seconds, it felt like forever before light bloomed from behind him and he smelled the welcome scent of fresh air.

He stepped out quickly and the group filling the alcove cheered.

"That was the coolest thing ever!" Colin shouted at his mother as Uncle Dan handed him down from his suit. Emmy was already standing next to her mother, gushing about their adventure so fast the words blurred together.

"Thank you so much for saving my children," their mother said to Carter.

"We didn't need saving," Colin insisted. "We were having fun!"

"We saved him from a pirate," Emmy added.

"And from weasels," Colin added. "We're heroes! Can we do it again? I want to see what it would be like if we smoosh together *Treasure*

Island . . ."

"And *Alice in Wonderland*," Emmy finished for him, making Carter shudder at the thought. "That would be amazing. Can we do it? Can we?"

The tired looking mother blinked as the children talked. "Not today," she said finally. "Maybe sometime."

All over the alcove, more kids began begging for a turn at the suits, tugging on their moms. They wanted to have a wild adventure just like Emmy and Colin.

"And he needs to come, too," one little boy said, pointing at Carter.

Carter held up his hands. "I'm all done with adventures today."

"I'm afraid all of us are done with adventures for today," Uncle Dan said. "We'll need to go over the system very carefully before we can use it again."

Some of the moms managed to drag their kids away then, while others came to Uncle Dan to ask if he would be coming back to the bookstore soon. Uncle Dan looked at them in surprise.

Isabelle stepped over to Carter. "Uncle Dan didn't think anyone would ever let their kids in a suit again after that."

"The kids had a blast," Carter said. "But I need a soda and maybe a nap."

Isabelle laughed. "We only heard some of it. The audio kept fuzzing in and out. You'll have to tell me all about it on the way home."

Carter turned to look at her, wide-eyed. "You mean you weren't following me every step?"

She shrugged. "We knew you'd do just fine. You're the best of all of us at this stuff."

Carter smiled. It wasn't often that Izzy complimented him. In fact, he couldn't really remember ever getting a compliment like that from her before. "Thanks."

Isabelle looked past Carter's shoulder and her eyes widened. "Well, I better see if Uncle Dan needs help." She backed away and hurried over to help her uncle disconnect computer parts.

Carter turned around and found himself face to face with Amber. "Oh, hi," he said.

"I'm sorry," she said.

"About what?"

"About acting like you were wimpy because of *Alice in Wonderland*," she said.

"That's okay," Carter said. "I guess I'm not really used to the books when everything goes right."

"You were fantastic," she said. "You saved those kids."

"The suits wouldn't have hurt them," Carter said. "The only danger really was dehydration if we left them in too long. And we could have cut them out of the suits long before that."

"I still think it was brave," she said. "I would have been scared to death, not knowing what might happen."

He laughed. "Well, I guess I'm getting good at the unexpected."

Amber looked down at her feet for a moment, then glanced back up. "So, do you think your

110

uncle might come back here with the suits?"

"If your aunt asks him, I'm sure he will," Carter said. "It shouldn't take him long to get the software all sorted out."

"Do you think you'll come back?"

"Probably," Carter said, feeling his cheeks warm. "I carry stuff."

"I hope you do," she said. Then she moved so quick Carter didn't have time to jump back. She kissed his cheek and then turned on her heel and dashed off through the store.

Carter looked after her, shocked. "Girls are weird," he said quietly. Then with a grin, he turned back toward his uncle and cousin to see if they needed any help.

Their first public outing with the virtual reality suits was a success, with only a slight problem after a power outage. Where will the suits take Uncle Dan, Isabelle, and Carter next?

Follow the adventure in

Book 6
A Novel Nightmare
The Purloined Story